P9-DEG-480

For Sam

First published in Great Britain in 2008 by HarperCollins Children's Books

Published in the United States of America in 2008 by Walker Publishing Company, Inc.
Distributed to the trade by Macmillan

For information about permission to reproduce selections from this book, write to Permissions, Walker & Company, 175 Fifth Avenue, New York, New York 10010

Library of Congress Cataloging-in-Publication Data
Chichester Clark, Emma.
Melrose and Croc : an adventure to remember / [Emma Chichester Clark].
p. cm.
Summary: A friendly crocodile receives the best birthday present ever when he rescues his dear companion, Melrose the dog, during a storm at sea.
ISBN-13: 978-0-8027-9774-2 • ISBN-10: 0-8027-9774-1 (hardcover)
ISBN-13: 978-0-8027-9775-9 • ISBN-10: 0-8027-9775-X (reinforced)
[1. Friendship—Fiction. 2. Birthdays—Fiction. 3. Dogs—Fiction. 4. Crocodiles—Fiction.] I. Title.
PZ7.C5435Md 2008 [E]—dc22 2007037146

Visit Walker & Company's Web site at www.walkeryoungreaders.com

Printed in China
2 4 6 8 10 9 7 5 3 1 (hardcover)
2 4 6 8 10 9 7 5 3 1 (reinforced)

Melrose and Croc

An Adventure to Remember

Emma Chichester Clark

Walker & Company
New York

In the early morning, as the sun rose,
two friends arrived at a villa by the sea.
“This is going to be your best birthday ever!”
Melrose said to Croc.

Croc looked around. “It’s wonderful!
You are such a good friend.”
“Just don’t look in any of the boxes!” said
Melrose. “I’ll be back soon.”

"But where are you going?" cried Croc.

"It's a surprise!" said Melrose.

"But I don't need any more surprises!" said Croc.

"This is a surprise you will really love."

Melrose smiled.

Down at the harbor, Melrose asked Pierre if he could borrow his boat for a little while. “Of course,” Pierre said, “but zere is a storm coming, so don’t be long.”

As Melrose rowed out to sea, he imagined the look on Croc's face when he gave him a fish for breakfast. He would be over the moon!

But Melrose didn’t notice how black the sea was,

or how dark the sky behind him had become.

While Melrose
was gone, Croc
explored the garden.
He picked a beautiful
bunch of flowers
for the table and got
everything ready.

Then he waited for Melrose. It seemed like ages.

Had something happened to him?

Suddenly Croc felt alone and afraid.

"I'll go and look for him," he thought.

But it was awful
outside. Rain was
pouring down as Croc
ran toward town.
There was no one to
ask—until he met
Pierre, who shouted,
"Zat crazy dog—'e's in
my boat! I told him,
'Ze storm is coming!'"
"Oh, no!" gasped Croc.

Croc ran at top speed
to the town binoculars.
Desperately he scanned
the stormy sea.

"Where are you?" he
cried to the wind.
"*Where are you?*"

And then, his worst
fears came true as he
saw a tiny boat with
a yellow dog inside it.

Croc ran to the lifeguard station.

"Help! Help!" he cried. "You've got to save my friend! Please help me save my friend!"

The alarm bell rang and all the men ran to the lifeboat.

Huge waves crashed onto the deck, jarring and cold, but Croc didn't notice. Suddenly he saw the little green boat.

"*There he is!*" he shouted. "Can we save him?"

"We'll do everything we can," said the lifeguard.

"I hope he can hold on."

"Melrose!" cried Croc. "Hold on, *please, hold on!*

We're coming!"

As the lifeboat came closer, a giant wave smashed into Melrose's boat and threw him out, into the sea.

Before anyone could stop him, Croc dived over the side of the lifeboat.

He held on tightly to
Melrose and swam
through the waves.
Then the lifeguards
pulled them up.

"Well done, little Croc!"
they said.
"You saved my life!"
gasped Melrose.

“I was so scared!” said Croc.

“But you were so brave!” said Melrose.

“I thought I’d lost you,” said Croc, and a tear slid down his cheek.

“I wanted to catch a fish for you,” said Melrose, “and now I’ve ruined your birthday.”

“Actually,” sniffed Croc, “so far, it’s the most exciting birthday I’ve ever had!”

As they came into the harbor, there were crowds of people cheering. Croc's eyes filled with tears again.

"Am I really a hero?" he asked.

"A real hero," said Melrose. "And a true friend."

SUPERCROC
we
love YOU!

They were presented with flowers and a beautiful fresh fish.

"Let's go home and open your presents!" said Melrose.

"But I'm so happy," said Croc, "I don't need any presents.

I have you *and* a fish!"

That evening, as the sun set, Melrose and Croc sat down to dinner.

“Thank you for being there, Croc,” said Melrose. “What would I do without you?”

“I don’t know!” said Croc. “What would I do without you?”